The Top Secret FILES OF MOTHER GOOSE!

BY **GABBY GOSLING** ART BY **TIM BANKS**

WALRUS BOOKS

For additional information, please contact Walrus Books,
351 Lynn Avenue, North Vancouver, British Columbia, Canada V7J 2C4

Edited by Kathy Evans at Walrus;
and by Gwen Strauss, Carina Chocana, and Lisa Bahlinger at Design Press
Cover and interior design by Design Press

Printed and bound in Hong Kong

National Library of Canada Cataloguing in Publication Data

Gosling, Gabby.

The top secret files of Mother Goose / Gabby Gosling ; Tim Banks, illustrator.

ISBN 1-55285-512-0

1. Nursery rhymes--Adaptations.   I. Banks, Timothy.   II. Title.
PZ8.1.G67To 2003   j398.2   C2003-910244-0

The publisher acknowledges the support of the Canada Council for the Arts and the
Cultural Services Branch of the Government of British Columbia for our publishing
program. We acknowledge the financial support of the Government of Canada through the
Book Publishing Industry Development Program for our publishing activities.

This book is dedicated to
the Savannah College of Art and Design
illustration students, whose work inspired this project.

ONE FINE MORNING,

the Queen of Hearts went down to the kitchen to fetch her breakfast tarts.

"My tarts are gone!" she cried. "I smell a rat."

Of course, that was impossible. The Pied Piper skipped town last year with the entire rat population and hasn't been heard from since.

The Queen gathered everyone from the castle to question them about the missing goods.

The King said he knew nothing about the tarts.

The Jester knew nothing about the tarts. All the King's men knew nothing about the tarts.

This left only the Knave of Hearts, suspiciously absent, and with a reputation as a tart-lover!

"It must be that pesky Knave again," said the Queen. "Off with his head!"

But no one knew where he was. One of the King's men suggested that someone call Mother Goose to track down the culprit.

That's me – Mother Goose, Chief Detective of Nursery Rhyme Crime.

I flew to the castle.

"So, Your Highness," I said to the Queen, "I understand
we have a situation with some tarts."

"A situation? I'll tell you the situation!
My tarts are gone!" said the Queen in a huff.
She was a little cranky without her breakfast.

"And no Knave, Your Majesty?"
I asked the King.

"No Knave," said the King.

"Any clues?" I asked.

"I'm clueless,"
said the King.

It wouldn't take a genius
to spot the obvious:
a trail of crumbs,
an innocent-looking dish
and spoon on the table
and a crumpled handkerchief.

"Hmmm," I said,
as I picked up the hankie.
It was embroidered
with a heart and the letters HM.

"Crumbs, a dish, a spoon
and someone's hankie.
        Looks like I need
        to find this Knave character and
            shake him down."

PRIVATE

CONFIDENTIAL

TOP SECRET

(Don't read past this point!)

I reached the Knave by cell phone.
Turned out he had a solid alibi.
He was in Hawaii on vacation.

"You have any idea who the rotten apple might be?"
I asked him.

"I wouldn't want to squeal," said the Knave,
"but, speaking of bad apples,
Mary Contrary might have some information.
Now if you will excuse me, I have a hula lesson!"

After I hung up, I thought about the Knave's lead.
Mary Contrary had a grudge against the Queen.
It all started with the strawberry festival last year.
The King and Queen were judges at the bake-off.
Mary tried to bribe the King with her strawberry tart,
but the Queen caught her red-handed.
She gave herself first prize instead.
Everybody knew it was a fix.
The way I figure it, Mary had a score to settle.

"Ever seen this dish and spoon, Toots?" I asked Mary
when I caught up with her.

"No, why?" she said innocently, tossing her head
and jingling her bells.

I told her about the Queen's missing tarts,
and Mary just laughed.

"Ever seen this handkerchief?" I asked her.
"Looks like your initial on it – M?"

Mary shook her head. "I've never seen it.
I don't know anything
about those tarts, honest."

I figured Mary couldn't have stolen the
tarts without someone hearing her bells.
Then I spotted what looked like
tart crumbs leading to Mary's stand
and beyond it.

"Thanks for your help, Doll," I said.

Mary Contrary

Rather grumpy. Mary runs a fruit and vegetable stand on the road into town. Wears silver bells on her clothes and eats lots of strawberries.

Favorite food: Home-grown vegetables

Criminal history: Former member of the Pretty Maids Gang

Following the trail of crumbs, I found
Miss Muffet practicing yoga on her tuffet.

"Does that hurt?" I asked.

"It helps me relax," she said,
"especially the pretzel posture.
Would you like me to teach it to you?"

She was a little too eager. I declined.

"Ever buy strawberries from
Contrary Mary's stand?" I asked.

"No, only blackberries.
I can't eat strawberries.
I'm allergic," she said.

"I see," I said. "By the way,
you didn't happen to lose this, did you?"
I asked, holding the handkerchief from the crime scene.

"Why no!" she said, jumping off her tuffet.
"Think of the germs on that thing!"

I thought she was going to fly the coop,
but she was just running to the kitchen cabinet.

"I prefer paper tissues! They're much more sanitary."

Miss Muffet pulled out a can of disinfectant and began
spraying the air around the hankie. I know her type:
she wouldn't eat tarts with just any dish or spoon.
It was then I saw the trail of crumbs
leading away from the tuffet.

"I'll be on my way, Miss Muffet," I said,
coughing through the cloud of
rose-scented disinfectant.

Little Miss Muffet

A yoga fanatic with a known fear of spiders. Also, a germ freak. And I'll bet my last dime that she doesn't eat sugar.

Favorite food: Curd cheese and sprouts

Known allergies: Strawberries, spider bites

The crumbs led me to Bo Diddle's place.
It was late in the morning, but Bo was barely awake.
Keeps musicians' hours, I guess.

"Mr. Diddle," I began, but he interrupted me.

"Call me Bo," he said, rubbing his eyes. "Man, what time is it?"

"Sorry to wake you, but I'm here on business
for the Big House. You know, Her Highness and His Majesty.
Now," I said, pulling out the dish and spoon,
"I know you recognize these two. What was in the dish, Bo?"

"Nothing at all, Detective Duck . . . er, I mean Chief Goose!
It was clean as a whistle!"

"I want the straight poop, Bo," I said.

"It's the truth, Ms. Goose! We were just having a little jam
session at the castle, you know, making music.
I used the dish and spoon to tap out a tune with Little Boy Blue.
He was there before me.
He might know what was in the dish!"

"Jam session?" I asked.
"Strawberry jam, by any chance?"

Bo Diddle just gave me a blank look.
My gut told me he wasn't our man.
But he got me thinking about
Little Boy Blue.

"He'll be asleep now. He sleeps all day,"
Bo Diddle informed me.

I thanked him, and flew off to
Blue's place.

Bo Diddle

Plays fiddle with the legendary band. Diddle. Diddle. whose last CD. "Over the Moon." went platinum in two days. According to one source. "Bo Diddle is one cool cat!" Seemed pretty much in the dark about the whole tart incident. Thinks Boy Blue might know something.

Habits: Often heard to remark. "Man. this place is jumpin'!"

Bo Diddle was right. Blue was still asleep when I got there. But not for long. He claimed he'd never seen the hankie. Under questioning, he told me he'd seen Little Bo Peep sneaking around outside the Big House the evening before.

"Maybe she knows something!" he said desperately.

"Maybe she did it, you mean?" I asked him.

He started to sweat. "I don't know. I'm no stool pigeon. That's your job," Blue said, as he walked me to the door.

I could see he didn't know a duck from a goose.
Still, he'd given me a hot lead.

Bo Peep was a little too easy to break.

"Miss Peep, I have an eyewitness that places you at the scene of the crime. What were you doing sneaking around the castle in the dark? Looking for a way into the kitchen?" I asked.

Her eyes sprung a leak and she started to sob. "I was only looking for my sheep!"

I pulled out the handkerchief, and before I could ask her about it, she took it and blew her nose with it. "That's tampering with evidence!" I quacked.

But it was clear to me that she was as innocent as a lamb. "Sorry to trouble you, Miss Peep, but I'm running out of leads."

Bo Peep looked up, sniffling. "Well, I know, there's, well, you might try the farmer's wife."

I told her the farmer's wife was missing. Peep hadn't heard this news. She looked like she might start crying all over again.

"It's those three blind mice! They were out to get her!" she cried.

"I know, Miss Peep. They're wanted for questioning. They're on the run. But that's another case."

"What about Patty Cake? He's a sworn enemy of the Queen," Peep said, wiping her eyes.

The lady had a point. If you were looking for someone who had it in for the Queen, Mr. Cake would top the list.

"I like the way you think," I said, as I flapped my wings and hurried off.

Little Bo Peep

Recent records show that the shepherdess has enrolled her sheep in a pet obedience training class.

Favorite food: B-a-a B-Q

Favorite song: Baa, Baa, Black Sheep

Habits: Cries easily and loses things a lot

Patrick Buttermore, alias "Patty Cake," the Irish baker. But, why would a baker want to steal someone else's tarts? It just didn't add up.

"What do you know about the Queen's missing tarts, Pat?"

Patty Cake smiled.
"Nothing at all, Chief.
Would you care for a sweet?"
he asked, pointing to a shelf full of pastries.

"Are you trying to bribe an officer of the law, Pat?"
I asked sternly.

His smile faded. "Of course not," he said.

"What do you have against the Queen?"
I asked, coming right to the point.

"Why, nothing. She's my best customer,"
Patty Cake said defensively.

"Don't play coy with me, Cake," I said.
"Everyone knows you don't like her. I want to know why."

Patty Cake blushed. "Truth is, I don't like that stingy Queen.
She always takes her sweet time paying her bill!
But she's my best customer for strawberry pastries.
I have to make so many strawberry tarts for her
and Peter Peter that I can't stand the sight of the
horrid things," he said.

"Peter Peter? I thought he ate pumpkins," I said.

"The wife eats the pumpkin," Patty Cake said.
"Peter Peter can't resist a strawberry tart."

I couldn't arrest Patty for just disliking the Queen.
I figured my next stop was Peter Peter's place.

Patrick "Patty Cake" Buttermore

Irish pastry chef known throughout the kingdom for his elaborate architectural cakes.

Dislikes the Queen.

Hobbies: Builds award-winning gingerbread houses

I found Peter Peter repairing a pumpkin shell.
"Patty Cake tells me that you're a fan of strawberry tarts,"
I said.

Peter Peter looked surprised. "No, not me, not me!" he said.

"Cut the double talk. I have proof that you buy
strawberry tarts – lots of them," I shot back.

"Well yes, but not for myself, not for myself!
I don't like strawberry tarts.
I buy them to give to the people who live in my pumpkins,"
he said. "I spend day and night, yes, day and night,
passing out tarts."

"Anyone see you giving out those tarts to your tenants?"
I asked.

I figured he wouldn't lie about giving away free desserts on
the night in question. I could check out his story easily.

"Sure, sure. Ask Humpty Dumpty, he got some.
He hangs out with all the King's men, you know."

I thanked Peter Peter for his help.

Peter Peter "Pumpkin Eater"

His odd name comes from a habit of repeating himself. Grows giant pumpkins in his garden and hollows them out to make houses for the poor.

Habits: He has a very generous nature

Close friend: Patty Cake— he gives him pumpkin meat for pies.

I tracked down Humpty Dumpty
at his favorite pancake hangout.
Dumpty cracked easily
under questioning.

"Yes! I know who stole the tarts!"
he sobbed.

"Tell me," I demanded.

"No! You can't make me tell!"
he blubbered.

Just then one of the King's men,
who was sitting at the table
behind us, approached.
I'd noticed that he had been
staring at the hankie I'd been
carrying as evidence and looking
worried.

"Excuse me, Ms. Goose," he said,
"but what are you doing
with one of the royal napkins?"

"What's it to you?" I asked him.

"Don't you know that's the King's linen? You can get in big
trouble for taking those from the castle!" he said worriedly.

Finally, it all started to make sense.
My guess was that this was an inside job.

Humpty Dumpty

A hard-boiled character.
Prone to accidents.
Spends much of his time
sitting alone. Can't seem
to pull himself together.

Close friends: All the King's
horses and all the King's men

Alias: Egghead

Known hangouts: Diners
and waffle houses

I realized that there was one person
who knew everyone in this story;
one person I had not yet questioned.
I quickly returned to the castle to confront him.

"One of your men tells me this belongs to you.
HM stands for 'His Majesty'," I said,
holding out the napkin.

The King crumbled.
He confessed to stealing his wife's tarts.

"It isn't fair!" the King cried.
"The Queen has wonderful strawberry
tarts, while my pie is always full of
four and twenty blackbirds,
and it tastes terrible!
I couldn't take it anymore!"

The King told me the whole sad tale.

He planned on eating just one tart
with the dish and spoon the night before.
But, unable to stop himself from eating them all,
he got scared. He snuck the remaining tarts
out of the castle and ate them on the run,
leaving a trail of crumbs behind him.

The King had some fancy
explaining to do to get back
in the Queen's good graces.
Under the circumstances,
I decided not to press charges.

The Queen forgave him —
eventually.

I will
I will
I will
I wil
not steal the Queen's tarts.
steal the Queen's tarts.
steal the Queen's tarts.
al the Quee

CASE CLOSED